The Queen Makes a Scene

Written by Mairi Mackinnon

Illustrated by Mike and Carl Gordon

How this book works

The story of **The Queen Makes a Scene** has been written for you to read with your child. You take turns to read:

You read these words.

Your child reads these words.

The Palace is sleeping, the moon is pale.

A light
in the night,
and a thin, sad wail...

Oo-oo-oo!

You don't have to finish the story in one session. If your child is getting tired, use the ribbon marker to pause and come back to it later.

You can find out more about helping your child with this book, and with reading in general, on pages 30-31.

The Queen Makes a Scene

Turn the page to start the story.

The Palace is sleeping,
the moon is pale.

A light
in the night,
and a thin, sad wail...

Oo-oo-oo!

The Queen has a pain!

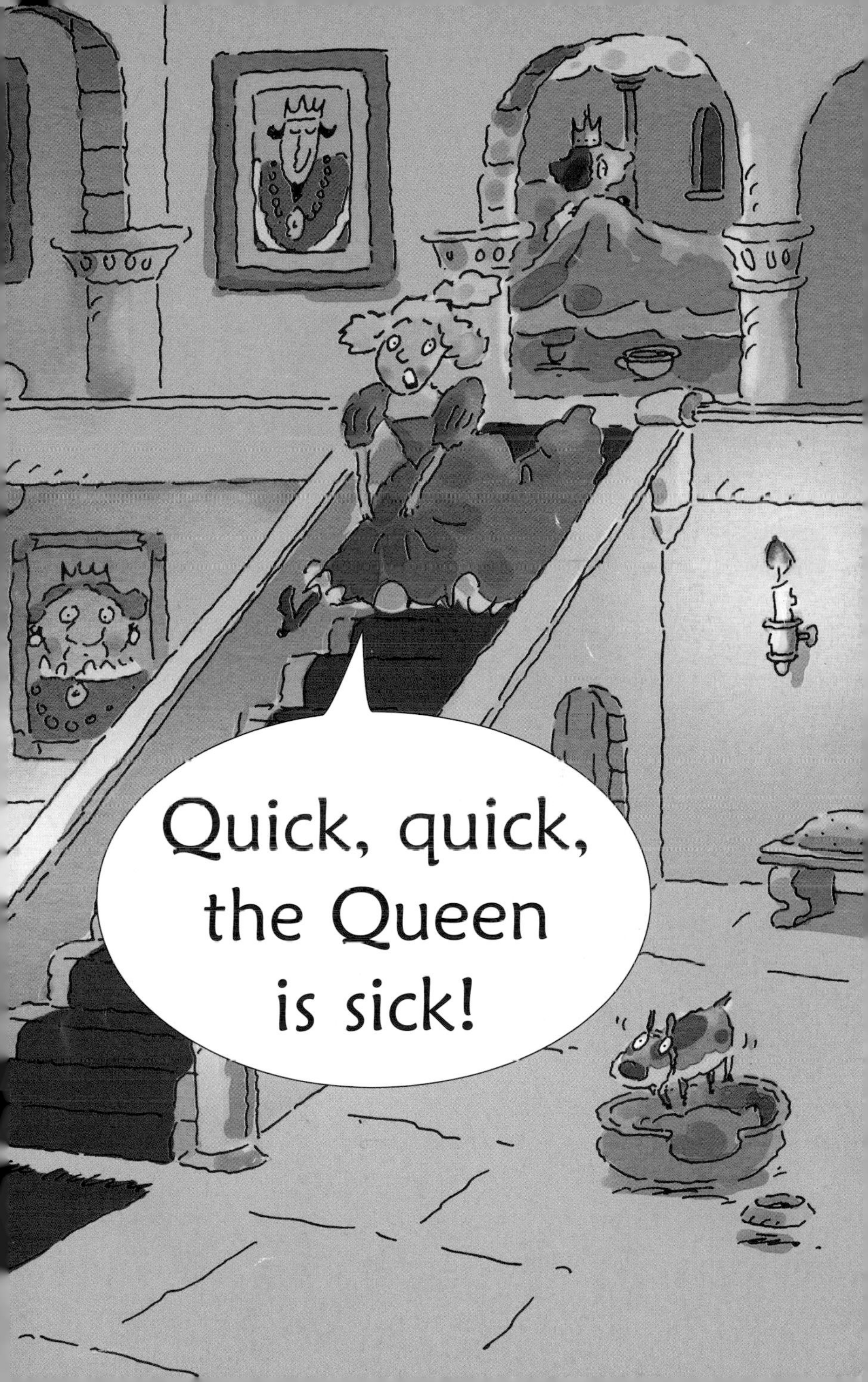
Quick, quick, the Queen is sick!

The maid calls a footman.
"We need Doctor Don."

"I can tell the Queen,
he will not be long."

Storm clouds are gathering.
The footman frets,

10

"I will need a coat,
I will get too wet."

The footman is in a terrible flap.

"Is this the right road?
I wish I had a map!"

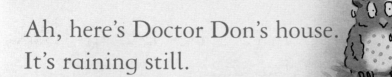

Ah, here's Doctor Don's house.
It's raining still.

16

"We need to be quick, the Queen is sick."

She cannot wait.

"Look, here is the doctor.
Go quickly, and tell..."

"But look at the Queen! She is up, she is well!"

She is not in pain?

The Queen is all smiles,
she says with a trill,

"I did feel ill, but
then I took a pill."

"And I feel right as rain!"

Puzzle 1

Look at the pictures, then choose
the right sentence.

1.

A **It is night.**

B **It is light.**

2.

A **"I will get too hot."**

B **"I will get too wet."**

3.

A "We need to be quick."
B "We need to be sick."

4.

A The Queen is ill.
B The Queen is well.

Puzzle 2

There is one wrong word in the sentence below each picture. What should they say?

1.

"The Queen is thick!"

2.

"I will need a goat."

3.

"Is this the right toad?"

4.

"I feel tight as rain!"

Puzzle 3

Find the words that rhyme. The first pair has already been linked as an example.

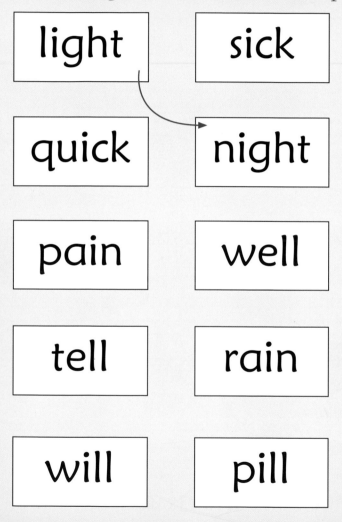

light	sick
quick	night
pain	well
tell	rain
will	pill

Answers to puzzles

Puzzle 1

1. A It is night.

2. B "I will get too wet."

3. A "We need to be quick."

4. B The Queen is well.

Puzzle 2

1. The queen is ~~thick~~!
   The queen is sick!

2. I will need a ~~goat~~.
   I will need a coat.

3. Is this the right ~~toad~~?
   Is this the right road?

4. I feel ~~tight~~ as rain!
   I feel right as rain!

Puzzle 3

light ⟶ night

quick ⟶ sick

pain ⟶ rain

tell ⟶ well

will ⟶ pill

Guidance notes

Usborne Very First Reading is a series of fifteen books, specially developed for children who are learning to read. In the first seven books, you and your child take turns to read, and your child steadily builds the knowledge and confidence to read alone.

The words for your child to read in **The Queen Makes a Scene** introduce these letter-combinations:

(Note that in standard English, oo can be pronounced either as in 'look' or as in 'moon' – both are used in this story.) It's well worth giving your child plenty of practice reading these. Later books in the series gradually introduce more letter-combinations and spelling patterns, while reinforcing the ones your child already knows.

You'll find lots more information about the structure of the series, advice on helping your child with reading, extra practice activities and games on the Very First Reading website, **www.usborne.com/veryfirstreading**

Some questions and answers

- **Why do I need to read with my child?**
  Sharing stories and taking turns makes reading an enjoyable and fun activity for children. It also helps them to develop confidence and reading stamina, and to take part in an exciting story using very few words.

- **When is a good time to read?**
  Choose a time when you are both relaxed, but not too tired, and there are no distractions. Only read for as long as your child wants to – you can always try again another day.

- **What if my child gets stuck?**
  Don't simply read the problem word yourself, but prompt your child and try to find the right answer together. Similarly, if your child makes a mistake, go back and look at the word together. Don't forget to give plenty of praise and encouragement.

- **We've finished, now what do we do?**
  It's a good idea to read the story several times to give your child more practice and more confidence. Then, when your child is ready, you can go on to the next book in the series, **Stop That Cow!**

Edited by Jenny Tyler and Lesley Sims
Designed by Russell Punter

First published in 2010 by Usborne Publishing Ltd., Usborne House,
83-85 Saffron Hill, London EC1N 8RT, England. www.usborne.com
Copyright © 2010 Usborne Publishing Ltd.

32

USBORNE VERY FIRST READING

There are fifteen titles in the **Usborne Very First Reading** series, which has been specially developed to help children learn to read.

To find out more about the structure of the series, go to **www.usborne.com/veryfirstreading**

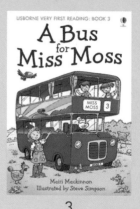

1

2

3

4

5

6